WEREDODO SLEUTH

EMILY MARTHA SORENSEN

Also by Emily Martha Sorensen

Standalones:
Black Magic Academy

Fairy Senses:
Fairy Eyeglasses
Fairy Compass
Fairy Earmuffs
Fairy Barometer
Fairy Pox
Fairy Slippers
Fairy Lunchbox
Fairy Icepack
Fairy Stopwatch
Fairy Toothbrush
Fairy Perfume

Dragon Eggs:
Dragon's Egg
Dragon's Hope
Dragon's First Christmas
Dragon's Fire

Comics:
A Magical Roommate
To Prevent World Peace

Picture Books:
Tabby, Tabby, Burning Bright

The End in the Beginning:
The Keeper and the Rulership
The Fires of the Rulership
The Magic or the Rulership

Trilogy of a Teenage Werevulture:
Trials of a Teenage Werevulture
Trifles of a Teenage Werevulture

The Numbers Just Keep
Getting Bigger:
Twenty-Four Potential
Children of Prophecy

Not Quite a Harem:
Not Quite a Curse

Magical Mayhem:
To Prevent World Peace
To Prevent Chic Costumes
To Prevent Clear Paths
To Prevent Smart Choices
To Prevent Warm Welcomes
To Prevent Cute Mascots

Short Story Collections:
Worlds of Wonder
Magic and Mischief

I know I put my car keys somewhere.

Weredodo Sleuth
Copyright © 2018 by Emily Martha Sorensen
Cover and internal art by Emily Martha Sorensen

ISBN: 978-1-949607-468

http://www.emilymarthasorensen.com

To Dorothy Gilman,

whose Mrs. Pollifax series
taught me that little old ladies
can make the best heroines.

Chapter Something

here was a crash.

I woke up, my heart pounding. *Is somebody trying to rob me? Did the heater explode? Did I leave the TV on all night again?*

Quite naturally, I had to investigate. What self-respecting weredodo would leave such a thing unexplained?

I hopped out of bed, slipped my feet into my fuzzy slippers, pulled on my bathrobe, which had a rather odd smell I couldn't quite place, and shuffled downstairs. I checked the living room, and everything looked fine. I checked the water heater, and nothing was different. I checked the kitchen, and everything seemed the same as I'd left it.

Except that my foot was cold. Why was my foot cold?

Ah. I had only put on one of my slippers, it seemed.

I stood there, puzzled, looking around the room. *Why did I come down here, again?*

I spun around in a slow circle, trying to figure it out. Surely there must be a clue somewhere.

The door! The door was ajar. I must have come downstairs to check the door!

Triumphantly, I headed to the kitchen door to close it.

Then I paused, puzzled.

Why had I left the door open? I didn't live in the safest neighborhood. I had forgotten to lock it before, but I didn't think I would have left it open. I thought back carefully. I hadn't gone outside yesterday. My clan leader had come to visit me, but she'd left through the front door, as she usually did. I vaguely recalled the back door having been closed last night . . .

Then my heart leapt in my throat. If I hadn't left the door open, then *somebody else must have.*

Sheer terror filled me, and I started to shake. Were they still in the house? Did they have a gun? I was only sixty-three! I was too young to be robbed at gunpoint!

No, no, I told myself. *Calm down. Calm down.*

I took deep breaths. All I needed to do was leave the house. If I told my neighbors what had happened, they would dial 911, and the police would come and take care of everything. They'd check my house to make sure the burglars were gone. I could go back to sleep, warm and secure and safe.

Or . . .

I looked around the room, my heart pounding with excitement. This was a genuine crime, wasn't it? I'd always wanted to be a sleuth. What self-respecting cozy mystery detective would let the police solve a mystery for them?

Oh, there were dangers, of course. I might be put in bodily harm. But on the other hand, my life had been so *boring* since I had been forced to retire early and my brother had started acting like an overprotective mother hen.

What self-respecting sister listens to her younger brother when he tries to act all authoritative?

My fear gone, replaced with glee, I pranced across the kitchen and flung open the back door. To my delight, there were footprints all over the snow outside, heading down the stoop and down the narrow path through my long-dead garden.

Let's see, I thought, squatting down and measuring one of them with my hand. *This is two and a half pointer finger lengths long.*

I should write this down. There was no way I'd remember.

CHAPTER Something

I reached into my pocket and pulled out a pen and a notebook. I scribbled down the measurement I'd taken from my first clue, made a carefully detailed sketch of the tread marks, and put the pen and notebook back.

I beamed as I stood up, my knees stiff from crouching. I was behaving like a real detective already!

There was a set of footprints heading clearly through the snow of my back yard. Not mine, I was certain, because my feet weren't as large as those. Besides, there hadn't been any snow on the ground when I'd gone to bed. The set of footprints made a detour to the kitchen window, and then over to the kitchen door, where I stood.

So the thief looked in the window before heading to the door, I deduced shrewdly. *That means he — or she — didn't come here knowing there was anything to steal. The thief just saw something he — or she — wanted, and went for it.*

Of course, that begged the question of what the thief had seen. What was in view from my kitchen window?

I shapeshifted into my dodo form and waddled around the large footprints so that I didn't disturb any evidence, wading through inches of snow to reach the kitchen window. I shifted into my half-form and craned my extra-long, feathery neck to see what the thief had been seeing from that position.

Aha! I thought. *The TV!*

I could just make out the TV in the living room behind the kitchen table. That had to have been their target!

Oh, wait, I thought, ruffling my neck feathers in embarrassment. *The TV's still there. So what did they steal?*

Maybe I'd left my wallet on the kitchen table. Had I left my wallet on the kitchen table? I checked my pocket, and my wallet was there, where I usually kept it, so that was good.

Well, this was most puzzling. Maybe nothing had been stolen from my house at all. That would be good, I supposed, but awfully disappointing. Being robbed would have been such an interesting change of pace.

And then I saw him.

The door to my coat closet opened slowly, and a man with a ski mask over his face poked his head out. His head whipped one way or the other, and he dashed for the kitchen door that I was standing beside.

I shrank until I was all-shifted and scuttled behind the box that belonged to the air conditioner's large outdoor fan, waiting with my heart pounding at triple the rate it should have.

I was little. I was tiny. I was only about three feet tall. He definitely wouldn't notice me here.

The man burst out of my kitchen door and ran down the path, snow flying as his boots churned it up.

One set of footprints, I realized with chagrin. *Of course he was still in my house. How could I miss such an obvious clue?*

Then the ski-masked man stopped abruptly. He looked at the bird footprints I had left in the snow. He turned slowly to follow them to where I stood, frozen in place.

I'm a statue, I thought. *I'm just a statue in a little old lady's garden.*

"Oh, come on!" he burst out. "You're clearly alive!"

I waddled over, pecking at the snow with large, innocent eyes. *I'm just a pet. A pet in a little old lady's garden . . .*

"Dodos are extinct!" he exploded. "You're clearly a shapeshifter!"

Ah. Yes. I might have forgotten that one small detail.

Deciding that I'd be a little more imposing if I were more than three feet tall, I shapeshifted into my usual human form, holding my hands out menacingly. "What were you doing in my house, sir?"

The ski-masked man stared at me incredulously.

Hmm. Perhaps my human form was a little less imposing than my dodo form, after all. I was a sixty-three-year-old woman in a nightgown. Also, it was cold out here without feathers. I tied the bathrobe shut in front of me, shivering.

"Okay, lady," the man said in what he must have thought was a reasonable tone, holding out his hands. "I didn't take anything. Got it? You're not going to call the police. Right?"

"Of course I'm going to call the police!" I said indignantly.

"Okay, look," the man said defensively, edging off to the side, "I didn't take anything. Okay? I just went in on a dare. There was a guy who gave me fifty bucks to do it. I'm not a thief, okay? Stop looking at me like that!"

I gave the man a stern look. "Being an accomplice after the fact still makes you guilty. Unless, of course, you'd rather be a witness instead."

He paused, looking right and left nervously. "Witness?"

"That's right," I said, drawing myself up to my full height. "I just so happen to be a sleuth. If you want to prove yourself not guilty, you can help me catch the person who did rob me."

"But I didn't steal anything!" he exploded.

"Ah, but somebody did," I said, raising my finger. I didn't know for sure if that was true, but I wanted it to be. "And so: who?"

He hesitated, looking one way or the other again, as if deciding whether to flee.

I folded my arms. "Are you familiar with my magical power?"

"Uh . . ." he said, eyeing me. "No."

"Well!" I said grandly. "Weredodos have the ability to track people wherever they go. If you try to leave, I'll simply call the police and lead them straight to your hideout. Your only option to prove yourself innocent is to help me find the real criminal."

The man's hand jerked towards his pocket, and I flinched back, terrified that he'd pull out a gun. In retrospect, I realized that killing me would also be a way to make sure he didn't get caught.

But he didn't pull out a gun. He just pulled out a wallet and threw a fifty dollar bill onto the snow. It lay there, fluttering slightly as a breeze drifted through.

"I got dared to do it," he said. "Just like I said. You can have the fifty dollars. Just don't call the police!"

For a moment, I considered it. Fifty dollars would be a reasonable reward for solving my first case, especially if no crime had actually been committed.

But if a crime *had* been committed and I let him go, I wouldn't be able to track my only witness. I'd been lying shamelessly about that. Weredodos had no magical ability.

Come to think of it, perhaps that was one of the reasons my species was so rare.

"You can keep it," I said grandly. "Don't be so silly. Pick it up before the thing blows away. Then come inside and tell me all about the person who dared you to enter my house. That person is now my chief suspect."

Looking very uncomfortable, the man in the ski mask picked up the fifty dollar bill and stuffed it into his pocket.

He headed back to the house with stiff shoulders as I followed after him.

I was about to interrogate my first witness. How exciting!

Chapter ?

y reluctant witness settled down as he seated himself at the kitchen table, looking most uncomfortable. Personally, I was delighted by this whole situation. Who would have thought this morning that tonight I would be on my way to solving my very own mystery?

"Now, first of all," I said authoritatively, "you must tell me your name."

"Sebastian," he said reluctantly. "Sebastian Noclanhuman."

Oh, that poor boy! I thought, pity rising. *His turning failed!*

My own turning had gone wrong when I was close to his age. I had been turned at twenty-one, back in the days before it'd been determined that seventeen was the optimal age, and instead of becoming a werehawk like the rest of my family, I had become a weredodo.

It wasn't that I minded being what I'd become. I had long since gotten used to it, and when most of my extended family members called me "Aunt Dodo," I was quite philosophical about it. Still, there was a part of me that wondered wistfully what it would be like to fly. Dodos were flightless birds, after all.

My heart went out to this poor soul who had come to my house. A failed turning was a nightmare. He would never be a person.

"Stop it!" he shouted, banging his fists on the table. "Stop looking at me like that! I *chose* to stay human, all right? I've never been turned on purpose!"

I blinked and stared in bafflement at this impossible young person who apparently lacked common sense in every possible way.

"Why would you stay unturned?" I asked.

"What's wrong with staying unturned?" he asked defensively. "My parents have never been turned, or the rest of my family either, and we're all just fine that way!"

My eyebrows raised. I lived only a few streets away from a human ghetto, so I had met humans before, but never one that had chosen to be that way on purpose. To be eligible for almost any well-paying job required one to be a person, seeing as most specialty fields required a magical ability that was unique to a specific race or species. For instance, most doctors were draculas, since they could use their blood to heal their patients.

"I would argue that you are not 'just fine' if you are so desperate for money that you think trespassing in somebody else's home for fifty dollars is a superb idea," I said mildly. "Now, tell me about the man who dared you. Do you know him?"

"No," the ski-masked man said immediately. "We were complete strangers."

Liar, I determined, and decided to write that down. I checked the pockets of my bathrobe for my notebook and pen, and found nothing. I checked my nightgown too, but there were no pockets within it. How puzzling. I could have sworn I'd put my notebook in a pocket earlier.

No matter. This was why I had a junk drawer. I kept spare paper and Post-It Notes and several dozen pens there in case I needed to remind myself of things.

I stood up and headed across the kitchen.

"Where are you going?" the human named Spencer demanded.

"I'm getting a notebook to write down your testimony," I said, pulling open my junk drawer. For a moment, I stared at the contents in bafflement. Why was there silverware in my junk drawer?

Oh, wait. My junk drawer was the one next to it.

CHAPTER ?

With relief, I opened the drawer to the right and collected a pad of Post-It Notes and several pens. I peeled off the top note, which said "Don't forget to pay phone b" and tossed it back in the drawer before heading back to the table.

"Now then," I said, sitting down with a purple pen posed over the block of sticky notes. "Do continue."

"Uh," the ski-masked man said, eyeing the Post-It Notes. "Uh, as I said, I have no idea who the guy was that dared me."

I wrote, *A likely story.* "Mm-hmm?" I asked encouragingly.

"I was just, like, out playing poker with my friends. I was on my way home, and . . ."

No-good gambling addict, I wrote. "Mm-hmm?"

"Oh, come on!" he exploded. "I can read what you're writing! I am not a gambling addict!"

"Well, then, I'd love you to explain why you were so desperate for money that you accepted a dare from a complete stranger to trespass in my house," I said severely.

He muttered something under his breath. "All right, my friends might've cleaned me out this week," he muttered. "Happy?"

I was, in fact. Interrogating a witness who was also a suspect was great fun. Not that I was sure what had been stolen, mind you, but I was certain there was something missing that was supposed to be in this room. Something . . .

I got up and headed to the wall.

"*Now* where are you going?" the man demanded.

"Nowhere," I said, adjusting the thermostat to 90 degrees. The vent was right behind the table. The heater immediately came on, and a wave of sweltering warmth gushed over us.

The man flinched and tugged the ski mask off his head.

"Aha!" I cried triumphantly, pointing at him. "Now I know what you look like!"

He froze, staring at the ski mask in his hand. Then he gave me an aggrieved look. "Lady, I told you, I haven't done anything wrong! I was just wearing that because it's cold outside!"

"Uh huh," I said gleefully.

He glared at me.

I studied his face, determined to be able to pick him out of a lineup if I had to. He had a thin nose, dark hair, no scars or freckles, a pasty complexion . . .

I sighed. Okay, I had no chance of picking him out of a lineup. He looked terribly boring, and if I was being honest with myself, there was no chance that I'd be able to tell him apart from fifty other young men like him. Still, he didn't have to know that.

"Now, then," I said, settling back into my seat, "tell me again about the man who dared you to enter my house. The truth."

"I told you the truth!"

"Then tell me again."

He looked like he was grinding his teeth. "I was just walking by —"

"In the middle of the night?"

"I was coming from a poker game with my friends."

"High school students shouldn't be playing poker," I scolded.

"I'm not a high school student! I'm twenty-five!"

"And still unturned?" I asked archly. "You're clearly sixteen."

"I'm unturned on *purpose*, lady!"

Well, why hadn't he said that in the first place? He did look a little old to be sixteen. I wrote *Unturned on purpose* on the top Post-It Note.

"Very well," I said, adding *Makes poor life choices* underneath it. "Please continue."

"Well, a man appeared from behind a lamppost and asked me if I'd like fifty bucks."

"You say 'appeared,'" I said. "What does that mean? Did he do it magically?"

"I don't know," the boy shrugged. "He was wearing black. It might've been magical, or I might've just not seen him."

Wearing black, I wrote down, reaching the end of the Post-It.

Why was I using a sticky note again? I ought to be using my notebook. I checked the pockets of my bathrobe for it, but all I found was a half-eaten sandwich. I sniffed it, wrinkled my nose, and set it on the table.

"How old is that?" the boy named Stewart asked in horror.

Chapter ?

"Not too old," I lied, though I had no idea. "But don't eat it."

He looked repulsed. "I wasn't going to."

Not always, I squeezed under the note that said *Makes poor life choices*.

"So the guy," Spencer said, "asked me, 'Hey, want fifty bucks?' I said, 'Sure. Why?' He said, 'I dare you to go into that house over there. The back door's unlocked.' I said, 'Why?' He said, 'My buddy bet me a hundred bucks I couldn't get someone to go into his house.' I said, 'Okay.' And I took the money and went."

I removed the top Post-It Note and wrote *Very stupid* on the next one. "Go on."

"Well, that's when I met you," he said defensively. "Can I go home now?"

No, he most certainly could not. Not until I knew what had been stolen, at least. Why did my kitchen look so wrong to me? Why did I feel like it was missing something?

I *knew* something had been stolen. And I had a feeling it had been something important. But what was it? What?

"What was the sound I heard?" I demanded. "The one that woke me up?"

"What sound?"

"The crashing one!"

"Ohhhh," Stuart said. "I dunno. I didn't make it."

"Did it come from outside?" I asked.

"I think so, maybe?" he hedged.

Maybe the crashing noise had something to do with what was missing from my kitchen. I stared around the room, focusing on each portion at a time, but nothing seemed to jump out at me. Everything was the same as usual.

This was maddening. I ought to be able to find out what was missing from my own house. I was a sleuth with the cleverness of a fox and a mind like a steel trap.

"Stanley, when you heard the noise —"

"It's Sebastian!"

Okay, like a sieve.

"— where did it sound like it was coming from?"

"I dunno," he said hesitantly. "Perhaps from . . . the right?"

My next door neighbor to the right were a childless couple from some sort of vampire clan. They weren't giants or specters. I could see no good reason why a crashing sound should have come from the direction of their home.

"Then we'll have to go speak to them," I said. "Come on."

"Come on where?!"

"To visit my neighbors," I said coolly.

"It's three in the morning!" he said shrilly.

"It doesn't matter," I said with great dignity. "They were most likely awakened, too. I am a sleuth, and so must investigate all clues. After all, a sleuth without clues is like a test without a student. Like a doghouse without a dog. Like a cookie without sweetness. Like a clan without a turning stone —"

I stared at the table and gasped. It had just clicked.

"What's wrong?" the boy asked, looking alarmed.

"My clan's turning stone!" I wailed in horror. "It's gone!"

Chapter Um . . .

h no. Oh no, oh no, oh no no. I remembered yesterday now.

Victoria was going to kill me. She was definitely never going to trust me again.

"Your what?" the human named Stewart repeated, his brow wrinkled as if he didn't understand the significance.

"Our turning stone!" I exclaimed. How could he, of all people, who had been through the terrible tragedy of having his turning fail, underestimate the importance of that? "I promised Victoria I'd watch over it while she was out of town! How could this happen?! She'll never forgive me!"

"Where was it?" Spencer asked urgently.

"On the kitchen table," I said, distraught. "I . . . I promised her I'd put it somewhere safe . . . but I forgot . . . and I must have forgotten to lock the back door, too . . ."

There was a terrible silence.

"So you told your clan leader you'd watch over your clan's turning stone, and instead, you got it stolen?" Summer asked.

"Yesssssss!" I wailed, putting my face in my hands.

He walked over and patted me awkwardly on the back. It didn't help, but I supposed I appreciated the gesture.

"Anabel couldn't have taken it," I murmured frantically, "because her grandson's living with her, and she doesn't want it at her house. Charles wouldn't have taken it — he would just have woken me up and scolded me. Irma wouldn't have taken it — she would have just hidden it someplace and left a note for me."

Just in case, I checked the floor, but there was no note.

"Who are those people?" Stanley asked.

"Charles is my younger brother," I said, getting up and checking a cupboard, just in case I had hidden the turning stone there. "Irma's my older sister. Anabel's in my clan."

"How many people are in your clan?" he asked.

I checked another cupboard. "Three."

"Isn't that kind of . . . small?"

"Don't rub it in!" I snapped, slamming the cupboard door. "We haven't had a new turning in forty years. I was the last one."

He wrinkled his nose. "Okay, I'm not an expert in clans, since I don't have one, but . . . isn't it kind of pointless to have a turning stone if you never use it?"

I opened the oven door. No stone within. "Do you think we don't want new members? Of course we do! But Anabel and I both came from turnings that went wrong, so neither of us have relatives who are interested in being dodos. As for Victoria, she quarreled with her children, so they all live in a different state and belong to a weredodo clan there!"

"Yeah, but if you're not *using* it, you might as well just *sell* it," Sonny said.

I spun around and gave him a furious glare. "Nobody would sell their clan's turning stone! There's always the *hope* of new members!"

"What if they could get a lot of money for it?" Sonny asked.

"Of course they could get a lot of money for it," I said tightly. "But your own clan's turning stone is priceless. It could never be replaced. Especially with a rare species, like dodos!"

"Because the stones have to be trained?" he asked.

"The word is 'programmed.' And yes. Our turning stone's been programmed over centuries to turn dodos. No one else could ever value it as much as we do."

CHAPTER Um . . .

I spun around, desperately seeking some other place I might have accidentally left it.

Aha! The dishwasher! I couldn't imagine why I might have put it there, but maybe . . . maybe . . .

No. There was no green, glowing stone.

A lump rose in my throat. This wasn't mere misplacing it. This wasn't like the car keys I'd lost two weeks ago and still not found. It really had been stolen. I really had carelessly allowed someone to steal it. I swallowed a sob —

No! No! I wouldn't let some selfish thief destroy my clan! I would stop them, and I'd find it!

I spied my phone on the countertop, and I seized it. I usually loathed my smartphone because I had a tendency to lose it, but right now, I was grateful for anything that could get me online.

"What are you doing?" Stewart asked, looking alarmed.

"Checking Wereconnection," I snarled. "Maybe there's another weredodo clan somewhere else in the country that is big enough that they want to split into two. They'd have a motive for stealing our turning stone —"

But there were too many clans when I searched for "dodo." There were hundreds, and at least five that had several hundred people in them. No suspects that would stand out to me.

Besides, was it really plausible that one of them had stolen my clan's turning stone? It was much more likely that it had been some common sneak thief who had simply walked by my house, seen the stone on the table, found the door unlocked, and walked off with it. Surely any turning stone could have value on the black market, even if it was programmed to an unwanted species . . .

I slammed my phone on the countertop. *An unwanted species!*

No. I would not let our turning stone be corrupted by another species. It was meant for turning dodos, and it would stay that way.

I had only one lead, and I would follow it. I'd solve the case, I'd save my clan, and I would show those no-good sneak thieves that crime never paid. That lead was . . .

Um . . .

That lead was . . .

What was that lead?

Maybe Skipper could help me remember.

"What else did you notice about the man who dared you to trespass in my house?" I asked him, turning around.

He stared at me, exasperated. "You mean, like the fact that he had a scar on his left cheek and he spoke with a heavy accent from south Paris and he was fairly obviously a dracula because he turned into a bat right in front of me?"

"Yes!" I exclaimed, diving for my Post-It Notes. "That will help immensely!"

"Do you know the meaning of 'sarcasm'?"

I paused, having gotten as far as "Almost certainly a dracula beca" in my notes. "What?"

"I was being sarcastic. I already told you everything I know."

I ripped the misleading Post-It Note off the top and wadded it up into a ball, preparing to throw it at him. The crinkling noise reminded me of . . . of . . .

"The noise!" I cried triumphantly. "We have to investigate that noise!"

Stanley looked less than enthusiastic. "There is no 'we.' I'm going home now."

"You most certainly are not," I said, fixing him with a stern glare. "You involved yourself in this crime, and now you have to help me solve it."

"I fail to see why," he said sourly.

I grabbed my phone from the countertop and held it up. "You want a reason why? I'll give you a reason why. If you leave now, I'll call the police and tell them that I caught you trespassing in my house right before I discovered my clan's turning stone had gone missing. Turning stones are worth hundreds of thousands of dollars, you know. Being involved in stealing one would be an automatic felony."

"C'mon, lady!" he cried. "You know I'm innocent!"

"I do not, in fact, know that," I said tartly. "But I do know your name, your face, and what neighborhood you likely live in."

Chapter Um . . .

He mumbled something under his breath.

"What was that?" I asked. "I didn't quite catch that."

"I said, 'Whatever,'" he muttered. "You could've used your tracking magic on me, no matter what."

What tracking magic? I didn't have tracking magic. I couldn't think where he'd gotten the impression I did. Still, it was a useful wrong assumption, so I wouldn't disillusion the boy.

"That's right," I said. "So let's stop wasting time. We need to go next door and interview my neighbors. Hopefully they saw something we've missed. Something that will crack this case wide open."

"Or maybe they were asleep. Like I want to be right now."

"Then we'll talk to everyone in this neighborhood!" I declared. "Someone must have seen something! We're going to find the thief if it's the last thing we ever do!"

Sonny looked dismayed.

"Well, come on," I said briskly, picking up my bathrobe. I pulled it on over my nightgown and tied it tight. "Let's go."

"You're going next door like *that?*"

"Indeed I am," I said. "I'm not letting you out of my sight. Unless you want to go upstairs with me while I change —"

"Please go next door dressed like that," he said immediately.

I smirked and went to the hall closet, where I retrieved a pair of snow boots. I put my phone in my pocket, in case I would need it again, then shoved my feet into the rubber boots. I walked back to the kitchen, where Spenser was thankfully waiting for me.

"How are you planning to explain me to your neighbors?" he wanted to know.

"Well, I was thinking I would tell them the truth —"

"No."

"Why not? If you have nothing to hide —"

"Just tell them I'm your nephew!"

I gave the boy a doubtful stare. Quite apart from the fact that we had no facial features in common, my skin was dark brown, and his was pasty white.

"I'll tell them you're my sidekick," I decided. "Every sleuth needs one, and I don't have a cat."

"How about assistant?" he asked.

"How about sidekick?"

"How about coworker?"

"How about sidekick?"

"I don't want to be a sidekick!"

"You'll do just fine," I assured him. "After all, you already have the perfect name for mystery solving."

"I what?" he asked, looking baffled.

"Sherlock," I said, shaking my head. How could he not know the name of the most famous detective of all time?

"My name is Sebastian!"

CHAPTER
It's on the Tip of My Tongue

Skipper did not look enthusiastic as I banged on my neighbor's door.

There was a long silence as we waited for someone to answer. I took the time to look out over the silent stillness of a snow-fallen night.

I could see our footprints in the blanket of whiteness, trailing from the front door of my house to our neighbor's. Shifting to half-form so that I could crane my extra-long neck, I looked back to see Sean's footprints heading behind my back yard towards the human ghetto, then turning to go into my house.

There was no sign of another pair of footprints back there.

I couldn't decide whether that made Sven seem more guilty, or whether that just meant the man he had talked to had been a specter. Specters could go insubstantial, after all.

But something was off about that . . . something . . .

Aha! I realized as the front door opened. *Specters can't talk while insubstantial! If the man were insubstantial, he wouldn't have been able to dare Sven!*

"H'lo?" the man asked in a bleary, grumbling voice.

I swallowed. I just realized that I couldn't remember my neighbor's name at all. Had it started with a P? Or a D?

"Hello, Mr. Vampireclandracula," I said, hedging my bets. "I'm your neighbor, Dorothy Wereclandodo."

"I'm not a dracula, I'm an aswang," the bearded man muttered, scratching his chin. "D'you know what time it is?"

"I believe it's three o'clock in the morning, but that's immaterial in light of the catastrophe," I said. "Did you hear a very loud crash about fifteen minutes ago?"

The neighbor's eyes opened beyond their sleepy squint. "What catastrophe?"

"The one in which my clan's turning stone was stolen," I said. "I very much need to get it back. Have you seen or heard anything?"

The man's eyes were now quite wide. "Your turning stone was stolen? There are turning stone thieves around?"

"Yes, I believe so," I said.

"Lily!" the man yelled, turning around to call up the stairs. "Check the safe! Check the safe now!"

So his wife was named Lily. That was helpful. I would have to remember that when I saw her.

"Mr. Vampireclanaswang," I said, "were either of you awakened by the crashing sound? I ask because I want to get right on —"

A woman screamed upstairs. Mr. Vampireclanaswang and I both bolted up there without hesitating.

At the end of the upstairs hallway was a safe. A safe that had been torn right out of the wall and flung on the ground. It looked like it had been punched open. And the safe was empty.

The neighbor woman, a forty-year-old showboat who tended to dress like she was twenty and wear layers of makeup so thick that they resembled a rock stratum, was now standing in the hallway in a silk nightgown and screaming.

I had a terrible misgiving that my turning stone had not been the only one stolen.

"What was in there?" I asked.

"Need you *ask?*" my neighbor shouted.

"Yes, I very well do!" I shot back. "I am a sleuth! I act on facts, not assumptions! Now: what was in your safe that is now missing?"

"What do you think?!" the man roared.

"Our — our turning stone," the woman sobbed, collapsing to the ground and staring at the empty safe. "Our clan's turning stone. How could this happen? Who would do such a thing?"

"I don't know," I said grimly, but a terrible fear rose in me. The last time there had been a rash of turning stone thefts, it had been because an underground organization had been stealing them to taint them, in order to blackmail the leaders of our city into . . . something. I didn't remember what offhand, but I knew my great-niece Lisette had done something to stop them.

What if my clan's turning stone has been tainted? I thought in terror. *It will have to be destroyed!*

That would be even worse than having it stolen and sold to become another clan's turning stone.

No. No, no, I told myself. *They fixed that problem, didn't they? They did. I'm certain they did. I would have remembered if they were still at large.*

"Bram, what'll we do?!" Lillian wailed.

"Yeah, looks really bad," Scooby commented from behind me. "That safe's totally busted."

I jumped. I hadn't even noticed that he'd followed me in, but of course he had. He was my sidekick.

"Who's that?" my neighbor snarled, pointing at Scooby.

"I'm her assistant," he said immediately.

"He means my sidekick," I corrected. "I am a sleuth, and he's helping me."

"Sleuth?" my neighbor asked sharply. I tried to remember what his wife had called him. Bran? Yes, it must have been Bran. "As in, detective?"

"Yes," I said firmly. "I'm here to solve the case, and I will do so. I'm quite certain the two crimes were perpetrated by the same people. Tell me everything you know or can surmise about what happened here."

"W-well," Lillian said in a wavering voice, "we keep the safe locked all the time. E-everybody in our clan knows we have the stone, but none of them would steal it."

"How often do you open the safe?" I asked.

"How often?" Bran repeated, as if I were speaking a foreign tongue.

"Yes," I said. "How often?"

"Whenever we have a turning," Lilith said in a shaky voice. "We have one in just a few days."

My mind hummed with that news. A turning in just a few days! Such a rare and special event, and they had one imminent. "So it's possible that it was someone was trying to prevent that particular turning. Your being about to use it in just a few days can't be coincidence —"

"Of course it can be a coincidence," Brian said brusquely. "We have a turning practically every week."

I gaped at him. "Every *week?*"

My clan hadn't had a new member in forty years. We were all over sixty. And they had a new turning every *week?*

I felt a stab of intense envy. It would be so nice to be part of a clan that was growing. Even a normal-sized clan, with a turning every year or so, would be terrific. I liked Anabel and Victoria, but our clan meetings were so desperately *boring*.

It was too bad Skyler's turning had failed, because I would have willingly invited him. Of course, I would have willingly invited anyone who could enliven things up. If he'd at least been unturned, perhaps I could have persuaded him to be a dodo.

"Yes, we have nearly a thousand people in our clan," Lina said, rising. She stared down at the safe and let out a moan of dismay. "How are we going to explain this to them? We can't possibly merge with another clan. Our meetings are too crowded as it is!"

I tried to feel sorry for them, and failed. Perhaps it was uncharitable of me, but the fact that merging with another clan might even be an option for them made me jealous. Our tiny clan had never had an option to merge with another dodo clan because of distance. The other dodo clans were all at least an hour away.

Bryan was giving Shaun a suspicious stare. "What does it mean to be a 'sidekick,' anyway?"

"Oh, well, we met because —" I began breezily.

"I'm her nephew!" Shawn said quickly.

Brandon looked at him. He looked at me. He looked at him. He gave me a flat look.

"He isn't my nephew," I said.

"You don't say."

"We met because —" I began.

"Because I'm dating her niece!" Shaun interrupted. "That's why I said I'm her nephew. I'm going to *be* her nephew."

I stared at him in horror. I certainly hoped he was lying. I might have been willing to allow him in my clan, but to allow him to date one of my nieces or great-nieces? Absolutely not.

"It's not really that serious," I replied with great dignity, figuring that covered all my bases. "You can't call me your aunt when you aren't even engaged."

"Just give us time," Stewart shot back.

"Um, excuse me," Libby said, looking from one of us to the other with a confused look on her face. "What is your name?"

"Sebastian Noclanhuman."

Libby gasped. "Your turning failed? Oh, you poor boy!"

"I hear there's a way to fix that now," Braeden said gruffly. "Some of the people in our clan have been talking about seeing if they can get work doing that if the process gets legalized."

"Which it shouldn't be!" his wife said indignantly. "It requires being tainted! Don't taunt the boy with things that can never be!"

"Those things very well *can* be," Bronson retorted. "There's a thriving black market right now. I imagine that's why our turning stone got stolen — so it can be used for that!"

Lilith let out a thin wail.

Oh, if only I had my notebook with me! Both Bronson and Libby were terrific suspects, but I wasn't sure I would remember all the reasons for it.

Bronson, of course, might have sold the turning stone to the black market in order to cash in on a fortune. If he made it look like a robbery, he might have thought his wife and clan wouldn't ever know he'd been responsible.

Libby, of course, might have wanted to protect the stone from clan members using it in the wrong way.

The two of them might have colluded on the scheme together. Or one of them might be trying to spite the other. There were myriad possibilities, and while I was sure neither of them could have pulled the safe out of the wall in that way, there was no doubt that they could have hired someone to do that.

Three suspects, I thought. *Bronson, Libby, and Skipper.*

While it was satisfying to collect new suspects, it wasn't enough to solve the mystery. A sleuth needed to do more than collect suspects: they also needed to eliminate them. And regardless of whether one of those three was the true culprit, there was clearly somebody else involved. Somebody with incredible strength.

"I think a giant did this," Lillian said, looking down at the safe, which looked like it had a hole punched straight through it. "Nobody else could, could they?"

I glanced up at the ceiling. It looked unharmed.

"No," I said with certainty. "Not a giant. A basajaun."

Everyone stared at me.

CHAPTER 4

basajaun?" Bruno repeated skeptically. "You mean the half-beasts?"

His wife elbowed him in the stomach.

"I mean the people whose physical appearance tends to resemble a were's half-form and whose racial magical ability is to become solider and tougher, yes," I said, ignoring the rude term. "A lot of giants could have done something like this, to be sure. But not without becoming taller than your ceiling. I see no cracks in it."

Everybody looked up.

"Now, a basajaun," I said, "can become solider and tougher at any time. They do it without growing larger . . . because of course, they can't grow larger, that being the giants' racial ability."

"What if it's not a racial trait, though?" Lilith asked. "What if it's a species trait that allowed them to do this?"

"Like what?" Seamus asked.

"A weregorilla," I said, catching on. "They're strong, even in human form. It's their magical ability."

"Eww." Lina wrinkled her nose. "A gorilla in my house!"

"A haltija," Brandon suggested. "They're super strong while insubstantial. That's why they guard banks."

Seamus pointed at the busted safe. "That was not done by someone who was insubstantial."

"Ghouls are pretty strong, and they don't feel pain," Lina said.

"True," Bruno nodded. "For that matter, draculas have super strength."

I was starting to feel rather dismayed. My suspect list, which had seemed narrowed down as far as one of the eight races, was getting broader and broader. Yet I couldn't afford to overlook these exceptions. Any one of them might be vitally important.

I had to take notes. I simply had to. I checked the pockets of my bathrobe, but I couldn't find anything there. Where had I put my notebook?

Maybe I'd take notes in my phone. I'd installed a program to help me keep notes straight a few months ago. Except, where was my phone? It wasn't in my bathrobe pockets, either! I thought for sure I'd brought it with me!

"At least we know what the crash was now," Skipperdoo said, pointing at the safe.

I nodded slowly. It *did* seem safe to assume that the crashing sound had come from this house . . . except . . .

"Except the crash didn't wake up either of you," I said to Bradley and Lina. "It woke me up, and I wasn't in this house. Are you both sound sleepers?"

"We woke up when you rang the doorbell incessantly," Braeden said sourly.

Which means it didn't come from here, I thought, nodding. *Which means . . .*

"Which means we have to check the outside again!" I cried. "There might be clues there we've missed! Skipperdoo, come with me!"

"My name is Sebastian! And it's cold outside!"

I ignored his protests as I marched down the stairs, and the rest of them followed me.

"I'm going to call the police," Brady said with an edge of defensiveness in his voice as I reached the front door. "No offense to your detective skills, but . . ."

"No, no, please call them," I said, waving my hand. "If I can't solve the case before they get here, I'm not much of a sleuth. If they can find our turning stones before I can, then I welcome their help."

Bruno nodded sharply, looking mollified, and then shut the door as Sassafras and I stepped outside.

"It's c-c-cold," my sidekick complained, rubbing his arms.

"You have a ski mask," I reminded him.

"I'm not going to wear it when the cops are coming!" he cried. "They might think I'm a crook!"

And yet, you didn't think anything of wearing it into my house, I thought, shaking my head. *Or of going into a stranger's house in the first place.* This human boy had such strange priorities.

Well, Spenser's complaining notwithstanding, I commenced a diligent search for clues. I hadn't thought to bring a magnifying glass with me, so I shrank down to dodo form and held my face close to the ground as I waddled beside Spenser's footprints, watching for any sign that someone else might have been outside.

We were almost all the way back to my house before I found the clue I'd been looking for.

"Just because he didn't leave any footprints doesn't mean I was lying," Steven was saying defensively. "He might've been a specter or something. He wouldn't have left footprints if he was insubstantial."

I had already thought of that theory, and dismissed it. Specters couldn't talk while insubstantial, much less hand over fifty dollar bills. If the man had been insubstantial, he couldn't have dared Steven or paid him to go anywhere, and if Spencer had lied about that, I had no reason to believe that there had been a stranger involved in the first place.

My eyes fell on a tiny scrap of something that looked like a corner from a candy bar wrapper.

I let out a quack of delight and shifted to half-form so that I could seize it triumphantly. It had been half-buried in the compacted snow of one of Stephen's footprints, which must have been why it hadn't blown away.

This was proof that somebody had been here, perhaps eating a candy bar while waiting for a gullible sucker to wander by!

Unless of course it was Steven's litter.

"Do you like candy bars?" I demanded, interrupting my sidekick's defensive and wandering spiel.

"Huh?" He looked startled.

"It's important," I said sternly. "Do you like them?"

"Ye-esssssss," he said slowly. "Everyone does. Why?"

"Do you like this kind?" I asked, shoving the tiny scrap at him.

Scotty stared at the corner of the semi-metallic wrapper, with its silver underside and brown top. "What kind is it?"

"A kind with a brown wrapper," I informed him. Was he blind? "Have you eaten a candy bar with a brown wrapper recently?"

"I — I have no idea," he said. "I might have. Why?"

"Because either this fell out of your pocket while you were walking . . . *or* . . ." I said dramatically, "it's proof that somebody else was here before you. It was partly buried in your footprint, which means you stepped on it."

Siegfried's face brightened. "Then it belongs to the thief!"

"Only if it didn't fall out of your pocket."

"It didn't," he said immediately. "It definitely didn't."

That didn't really strike me as convincing, given that he had only declared himself sure that it wasn't his after I had told him it would prove his innocence if it wasn't, but never mind. It might still be useful. Any slight lead was better than nothing.

I shrank back to dodo, not bothering to pocket the clue because it would disappear inside me, like my clothes, while I was shifted. I found nothing else beside Spaghetti's footprints, so when they veered off towards my house, I kept heading straight forward.

"Hey. Hey!" Squirrel protested. "Where are you going? The warm house is that way!"

I turned around and shook my feathered dodo head in disbelief. Did he really think we were done searching for clues?

"Warm house!" he insisted again, pointing.

I shifted back into my human form, now holding the tiny scrap of clue in my left hand, where it had been before I'd shifted.

"Sheridan," I said patiently, "the crash might have come from the other side of my house. We need to talk to my other neighbors."

"Sebastian," he said. "It's Sebastian. How bad *is* your memory?"

I ignored that terribly rude question. "We probably don't have much more time before the police come, and I'd dearly like to solve this mystery before they get here. Come on."

I shrank to dodo and continued waddling forward through the freezing powder.

He grumbled vehemently as he stomped after me. I didn't know why he was the one complaining. I was the one wading through inches of snow wearing nothing but feathers and bare bird feet.

When we reached the side yard of my right neighbors' house, I spied something that presented a dreadfully disappointing solution to the mystery of the crash.

I shifted to my half-form so that I could sigh heavily.

"What?" Siegfried demanded. "What is it?"

"Their garbage cans are lying on their sides," I said, pointing. "With the trash scattered everywhere. The wind must have blown them down."

"So . . . the crash didn't have anything to do with the robbery?" he asked.

"Apparently not." It was most disappointing. "I suppose I should be grateful that the noise woke me."

"You should," Sheridan said. "You definitely should."

"I suppose so," I said desultorily. "But now one of my clues is gone."

"Not all of them," Sheldon said. "You still have . . ." He stopped and stared at my empty fingers. "You didn't drop the thing that proves my innocence, did you?!"

I laughed and shifted all the way back to human form. The clue reappeared in my fingers. Trust a human to be ignorant about how weres worked. "No, no. I just made it disappear inside me while I shifted. Weres can do that."

"Only with their clothes, though, right?" Shelly said.

"Of course not," I said. "We can do it with anything, within reason. For instance . . ."

I grabbed a loop of his jeans before he could stop me, and shifted to dodo. He was left standing in the snow in boxer shorts.

"HEY!" he shouted.

I snickered as I shifted back, and his pants reappeared. "It was just an example."

"A VERY COLD example!"

Spencer did not seem particularly happy. I, on the other hand, was quite impishly amused.

"Very well," I told him. "Let's go back to the house. I'll make you some ginseng tea to warm up."

"I want hot chocolate instead," he complained.

CHAPTER 4

ust because he wanted hot cocoa didn't mean I had any. My great-niece Annette had drunk all of it the last time she'd visited.

"You're going to love ginseng tea," I assured him, putting the kettle on the stove and heading back to the table. "It's delicious."

"Aren't you supposed to turn the stove on?" he asked.

I paused, then ran back to do so. "Of course. I was just testing to see how good your detective skills are. Sometimes I wonder why your parents named you Sherlock."

"They didn't!"

"In any case," I said, seating myself at the table, "we need to figure out how the man who left this clue did not leave any footprints. Was he hovering over the snow?"

"I dunno. I wasn't looking."

"Did he have wings?"

"He was wearing a jacket."

I sighed. Sherman was not being very helpful.

"How tall was he?" I asked.

"Average height?" Skipper hedged.

"Short end of average or tall end of average?"

"I wasn't paying that much attention! What does it matter?"

"If he was on the shorter end of average," I said reproachfully, "he could have been a very tall abatwa, such as a pixie or sprite."

"Well, I don't know," he snapped, "so it doesn't matter."

Another useful possibility occurred to me. "What color was his skin?"

"What does that matter?"

I stared at Sumner in exasperation. One might suspect him of being deliberately unhelpful. "Just answer the question."

"I dunno. Medium, I guess."

"Medium brown, or medium peach?" I asked, gesturing from my dark wrinkles to his pale pastiness.

"Medium peach?" he hazarded.

So that was another possibility eliminated. Tellems were a species of abatwa that could fly without wings, but they all had brown skin, even if they had been white before being turned.

"It might have been a kappa," I mused. "They can control water, including snow. If it was a kappa, he might've erased his footprints."

"What if it was a plain old, boring human?" Silas demanded, looking annoyed. "Why does it have to be someone with magical powers?"

"Oh, Sirius," I said, shaking my head. "You do realize that if I thought a human had done it, you'd be my prime suspect?"

"Why *couldn't* a human have done it?" he asked defensively. "We're smart, too!"

"Smart, yes, but capable of walking on snow without making any mark in it, no. It's possible the thief came to my house before the snow fell, but in that case, he couldn't have left the clue. The clue was only partly buried in your footprint, which means it was on top of the snow when you stepped on it."

"So maybe someone else left the clue," he said. "Maybe the thief came hours before the snow fell."

"Then why did someone dare you to come into my house?" I challenged. "If nothing else, the person who made that dare was standing out in the snow without having left footprints."

"Okay! Whatever!" he said, throwing up his hands. "At least my being human means I'm innocent, then!"

"Simon, you *did* leave footprints leading up to my house," I said with exasperation. "Your being human proves no innocence at all. Now, maybe if you were unturned as opposed to having had your turning fail . . ."

"Why would that make a difference? And I *am* unturned! I told you that before!"

Had he? I didn't remember.

"Well, in that case," I said, "I highly doubt that you would have stolen a turning stone, much less two of them. The very fact of what was stolen implies your innocence."

"Huh?" he asked.

"If an unturned human touches a turning stone, they turn immediately," I said. "If they do so without anyone else touching it at the same time to show the stone the desired form, the turning usually goes wrong or fails. That is, of course, why turning stones are rarely kept in the same house with small children. If you are unturned, I doubt you'd want to take the chance of stealing a turning stone and perhaps possibly touching it by mistake."

Samuel shuddered.

"Exactly," I said. "Now, a human whose turning had failed might be an excellent suspect, if only the evidence didn't imply magic being used. A human whose turning had failed might have a possible motive of wanting to spite people whose turnings had succeeded . . ."

My voice trailed off. What if Silas was lying about his unturned status? I had the sudden, uneasy feeling that I had forgotten the rather obvious possibility that more than one person could have been involved in this robbery.

I silently ran through the possibilities in my mind. If he was guilty, then he must have hidden the turning stone somewhere in my house. He couldn't have delivered it to anyone else, because I'd been watching him ever since I'd found him. He couldn't be carrying it on him, because turning stones were quite large — the size of a bowling ball.

As I was starting to worry extremely that perhaps I had made a dreadful miscalculation, I heard a knock on my front door.

I jumped, startled.

"Police!" a voice called. "Ms. Wereclandodo, may we speak with you?"

"Oh, good," I said with relief. I'd wanted to solve the case before they came, but now I was more worried about my safety. "Sherwood, come with me."

"What am I, Robin Hood?" he grumbled. But he got up from the table and followed me to the front door.

I opened it and let two police officers in. One of them, a man with a dog face, tipped his hat.

"I heard about your loss, ma'am. May we investigate your house to see if we can find anything of help?"

"Of course," I said.

He immediately became a tailless dog with a man's face and raced down the hallway, sniffing with his nose to the ground.

"What's that?" Stanford demanded, looking freaked out.

"He's a penghou," the other police officer said, chuckling. "He can sniff out turning stones, among other things."

"Is that some kind of weredog?" Stanford asked.

"No, it's a kapre. He can also turn into a camphor tree."

Kapres were like weres, except that they shifted into plants instead of animals.

"But he's a dog!" Stanford exclaimed.

The other police officer laughed heartily. "Well, in that case, I'm no more than a horse."

"What species are you?" I asked curiously.

"A nokk," he said. "I turn into a horse when touching water."

I couldn't quite remember which race they belonged to. "A specter?" I hedged.

"Lorelei."

I blinked. All loreleis could only breathe underwater during the full moon. "So you spend your full moons as a horse surrounded by fish and mermaids?"

"Yes, I do."

His partner ran back, tailless rear end wagging, and he turned into a human with a dog face again.

"Smell anything?" the nokk asked.

"No turning stones here," the penghou said.

"What about insubstantial ones?" I demanded. Because it had occurred to me that Simon might have been lying about being human. He could be a specter who had hidden my turning stone in a wall.

"I'm getting to that." The penghou cracked his knuckles, stretched, and shifted into a short, spindly camphor tree. A branch shook vigorously, and a leaf broke loose and fell onto my carpet. A second later, he was back to being a man with a dog face. He leaned over and picked up the leaf.

"Does the leaf help?" I asked in confusion.

"The smell of camphor makes it possible for me to sniff out insubstantial things," he explained, pulling a rubber band out of his pocket and stretching it around his head to fasten the leaf on top of his nose. "Be right back!"

And the man-faced dog raced off through my house again.

"While we're waiting, why don't you tell me how you figured out your turning stone was missing?" the nokk asked me, pulling a notebook and pen from his breast pocket.

I eyed the notebook enviously. If only I knew where I had put mine.

"Well, it all started when I heard a crashing sound," I began.

Come to think of it, we still hadn't found any explanation for that noise yet, had we? I would have to take Sirius to investigate. Maybe my neighbors to the right had heard it. I really should have thought to go there while we were still outside.

"And then I went downstairs, and I found —"

Severus let out a protesting sound.

I turned to give him a disapproving stare. If he was innocent, he shouldn't mind me telling the police the whole story. We had to catch the crook.

"Yes?" the nokk police officer asked.

He was interrupted by a loud whistle from the tea kettle.

I jumped, my train of thought completely interrupted. What was that horrible noise?

"Is that the teapot?" Saul broke in eagerly, looking relieved. "We're making ginseng tea. You want some?"

"No, thank you," the nokk said.

"It was ginger tea," I corrected the boy.

"No, it was ginseng."

"Ginger!"

"Ginseng! She has a terrible memory," Stetson added in a confidential whisper to the police officer. "That's why I'm here. To help her. I'm her assistant."

I bristled. "The word is 'sidekick.'"

"The word's 'assistant.'"

"No, it's 'sidekick'!"

"See?" Stetson said, shaking his head. "Terrible memory."

I was very annoyed.

CHAPTER 4

We headed back to the kitchen to check on the tea kettle. It was whistling quite shrilly as it waited for us.

"Hey," Sampson whispered as I lifted the kettle off the burner. He eyed the hallway where the nokk was standing. "Don't tell them about how you met me."

"I certainly will," I said, turning off the stove. "You should have nothing to hide."

"I don't wanna get thrown in jail for trespassing!" he hissed.

"Well, maybe you should have thought of that before you took that silly bet."

"It was a dare, and I regret it, okay?"

"I'm glad to hear that," I said. "But you're still the only witness who has seen the man who probably broke into my house. You need to tell them the whole story so that they can find him."

Sawyer ground his teeth. "I don't know anything useful."

"I imagine they'll be the judges of that."

"I don't want to get in trouble!"

"I'm delighted to hear that. I'm sure you'll behave with more wisdom in the future."

He glared at me.

"Is there a disagreement here?" the police officer from the hallway asked, wandering into the kitchen.

"Yes," I said. "Sawyer's being a little silly. If you don't like ginger, can I get you another kind of tea? I have ginseng and chamomile."

"No, thank you," the police officer said. "I'd rather not turn into a horse right now. Can you tell me about how you found your turning stone was stolen?"

I stared at him. Good gracious! A horse? Why would that happen?

"Hey, how come you guys aren't next door?" Sonny broke in. "Their turning stone was stolen, too."

"We have another unit over there," the man who had been inexplicably worried about turning into a horse said. "Right now, we're here to help you. Please tell me how you learned the stone was missing."

"Well, there was a crashing sound," I said, "and then —"

"I was here with her the whole night," Sawyer broke in. "Because I'm her assistant."

"You'll get your chance to talk, son," the police officer said, looking rather annoyed. "Let me hear from her first."

I blinked in startlement. "Is he your son?"

"What?" the police officer asked, looking baffled. "Oh, that. No. It's an expression. Please go on, ma'am."

I cleared my throat. "Well, it all began when there was a crashing sound from outside . . ."

I went on to explain everything else that had happened so far, stopping a few times to fill in parts I had forgotten. As I did so, I poured the water from the tea kettle into the mugs for me and Spencer, and I passed one to him. I sipped mine, which tasted rather flavorless for some reason, as I talked.

The police officer said nothing aside from "Mm-hmm" and "Uh huh" and "Go on" while he wrote down my words, and it wasn't long before his partner joined us, asking for permission to open anything that was currently shut.

"Of course," I said. "Please search everything."

By the time I finished my story, he was back, having searched everywhere thoroughly.

"No turning stones," he said, "substantial or insubstantial, though there was one on this table recently."

I sighed. So much for my last vestige of hope that I had simply hidden it somewhere I'd forgotten. Still, that also cleared Sherwin. It was rather a relief to know I hadn't been spending the last two or three hours with a criminal.

"Sorry, ma'am," the non-canine police officer said. "Quite often missing turning stones turn out to still be hidden insubstantially in the house they went missing from, but it seems this time that isn't the case."

"Quite often?" I asked. "Do turning stones get stolen a lot?"

"More often than you might think, given how careless people can be with them. That's why we have officers specially trained in hunting them down."

"Me," his dog-faced partner said, raising his hand cheerfully.

"But that wasn't even what I was talking about. It's far more common for a specter to accidentally turn one insubstantial and knock it inside a wall or under the ground. You'd be amazed how many times that's happened."

"So you thought it might be accidental?" I asked.

"Indeed," he said. "It happens all the time with senior citizens, especially specters."

I bristled. "I am not a specter! And I wouldn't misplace such an important thing!"

"Of course not," he soothed. "May I ask what you are?"

"A weredodo," I said.

He and his partner exchanged a glance.

"Are you in half-form, by any chance?" the dog-faced man asked delicately.

"No, I am not!" I said indignantly. "I wouldn't disappear an entire turning stone inside myself without noticing! And do I *look* like I'm in half-form?"

"Half-forms aren't always obvious," the dog-faced officer said. "I have a sister who's a weredog. As long as she keeps her hair combed over her floppy ears and her paws in shoes while she's half-shifted, nobody notices."

"Well, *my* half-form is obvious," I said huffily, demonstrating. An enormously long feathered neck sprouted between my head and shoulders.

"No offense meant, ma'am," the non-canine assured me. "It's just that penghous can't sniff out turning stones that are hidden inside weres. And we've seen it happen before. Especially with senior citizens."

I was getting extremely irate with his use of that word. Some might think that knowing how age had degraded my memory would mean I wouldn't mind others assuming that fact. But no. That just made it even more of a touchy subject. Especially when there was any implication that I might not be competent enough to take care of myself.

"Well, I appreciate your checking every possibility," I said coldly. As far as I was concerned, the two police officers had now worn out their welcome. Polite about it or not, I did not entertain strangers questioning my judgment. I got enough of that from my brother. "Now that you're satisfied that I was not the accidental culprit, I hope you'll be able to find the thief before he gets much further away with my clan's turning stone."

"Just one last thing," the dog-faced man asked, eyeing Sherwin. "What species are you?"

"Human," he said with an edge in his voice.

"I don't smell a failed turning," he said suspiciously.

"You wouldn't! I'm unturned!"

"Hmm. That would explain it." The dog-faced man paused. "How old are you, kid?"

"Twenty-five."

"And still unturned?"

"Yes! I'm allowed to stay unturned if I want to!"

The dog-faced man scratched under his neck. "Sure, you're allowed to, kid, but it's pretty weird."

Sherwin looked very peeved.

"Oh, here's the clue we found outside," I said, remembering it for the first time. I picked it up from the table and handed it over, explaining where we'd found it and what we'd deduced from it.

"Perhaps you can check it for fingerprints!"

"Perhaps," the non-canine said, pulling out a plastic bag and gesturing for me to drop it in. He didn't seem to consider my clue particularly revelatory. "It might have been more helpful if you had left it where it was."

"She couldn't do that!" Sherwin said defensively. "The thief might have come back and picked it up to cover his tracks!"

"Uh huh." The police officer looked like he didn't believe for a second that would have happened. "Well, thank you very much for your help. We'll get back to you as soon as we find your stone, or if we have any other questions."

"You *will* find it, right?" I asked anxiously.

The non-canine police officer paused. "I'm not going to lie to you, ma'am. In cases like this, where the object wasn't simply misplaced and we have no solid leads, the chances are only twenty, thirty percent that we'll find it eventually. We'll do our best, of course, but you might have to accept that it's gone."

That took the breath out of me. Even the police couldn't promise any more than thirty percent?

No. That wasn't acceptable. I couldn't let it be gone.

"Thanks very much for your time," the dog-faced man added, bobbing his head with his ears flopping.

The two of them got up and headed to the front door.

"You're welcome," I said quickly, following them, "but I can help much more than this. I'm a sleuth. I can find more clues —"

"Of course," the non-canine said. "Give us a call if you find any."

I had the nasty feeling he was only humoring me.

"I *can!*" I said angrily. "I can, and I *will!*"

"Well, then, remember to leave them where they were, so we can inspect them properly," the dog-faced man said, tipping his hat. "Good day, ma'am."

As the front door shut, my blood was boiling. I wanted to be taken seriously, and I would be. I was certainly not going to trust the fate of my clan to the police's twenty percent. If they weren't going to find it, I would do it myself. I had wanted to do that, anyway.

I sipped my flavorless tea, fuming. Surely I had learned something earlier that would crack this case wide open. That was how mysteries worked. All I had to do was put the pieces together in the right way, and the answer would emerge from a chrysalis, flapping its wings in brilliant obviousness. I just had to notice something . . .

Something . . .

Something . . .

Blast. Nothing was coming to mind.

"It's a shame about your turning stone," Shelby said.

I ignored him. This wasn't a time for my sidekick to distract me. I focused all my brainpower on sorting through tonight's clues.

"I know you wanted it," said Something. "But really, is this so bad? I mean, you weren't using it. If no one's joined your clan in forty-two years, it's highly unlikely that . . ."

Yammer, yammer, yammer. I wished Something would cut it out. Couldn't he see I was trying to think?

There was something about that safe that bothered me. The way it had been ripped out of the wall and punched through, with no noise being made. I was pretty sure I knew what species could do something like that, if only I could . . . remember . . .

That's it! The answer burst into bloom in my mind.

I stood up from the table, drank the rest of my lukewarm tea in one gulp, and slammed the mug on the table. "Come on, Shannon! We've off to investigate!"

"Off to investigate *what?*" he goggled.

I grinned ferociously. "The Vampireclanaswangs' safe. I'm about to blow this case wide open."

Wasn't This Chapter 4?

I marched steadily forward, heedless of the powder I was kicking up as we went. I didn't even worry about the tiny flakes drifting down from the sky. If I was right about my theory, and I was guessing I was, it wouldn't matter if the footprints were all erased.

Sheldon let out a steady stream of grumbling from behind me, mostly about the fact that I had refused to elucidate him before sending us back out into the cold.

"Just be patient!" I called, not turning around. "I can't explain until everybody is there at once!"

Honestly! Hadn't he ever read mysteries?

"But do you know who *did* it?" he yelled.

"All will be revealed!" I called back mysteriously.

We reached the front door of my neighbors' home, I pounded on it, the door was opened, and the Vampireclanaswangs were more than a little surprised to see us back.

"We have the police here," Lillian said. "We don't need you."

"There's where you're wrong," I said. "I've noticed something that everyone else overlooked."

"Are you all right?" Braden asked, glancing behind me. "You look a little ill."

"So c-cold outside," Stephan complained.

"Well, come in, then," Layla said, looking displeased to be forced into hospitality.

I didn't wait to be invited twice. I immediately bustled in and up the stairs, fairly relieved myself to be back in a warm house. In my excitement, I had found the flurries and the chill wind simulating rather than upsetting, but there was no denying that my ears felt like two ice cubes hidden in an igloo and then packed with snow to keep a soda can cold.

Upstairs, I found four police officers pouring over the broken wall and the busted safe, talking to each other and taking notes. Two of them were the ones who had been at my house before.

"Hey!" the dog-faced man said, alarmed, as I headed toward them. "Stay away from the crime scene!"

I ignored this advice, though I stopped short of coming close enough to disturb anything they were photographing.

"Is everyone here?" I asked, looking over my shoulder.

The Vampireclanaswangs emerged from the top of the stairs. Sinclair was with them, shivering as he hunched into the scarf Lilith was draping over him.

"What is this regarding?" one of the police officers I didn't know asked, looking annoyed.

"It's regarding the fact that I know exactly what species did this," I said proudly, pointing at the safe and then the wall it came from. "It's a haltija."

The police officers didn't blink.

"You don't say," said one of the unfamiliar ones. He was a duergar, and very ugly.

"You see, haltijas only have super strength while insubstantial," I said excitedly. "So we figured one of them couldn't have done this. But a specter can also make things they touch insubstantial at any time! Which means he could have made the safe and the wall insubstantial, ripped the safe out of the wall, punched it open, grabbed the turning stone, and escaped! It could all be done in complete silence, because insubstantial things don't emit sound waves!"

My brilliant theory was met by stormy silence.

"This is not our first haltija crime," the duergar said finally.

I blinked and stared at the four police officers. They all looked rather impatient.

"Is there anything else?" the non-canine who had been at my house asked.

"Um . . . yes!" I said, as a new idea occurred to me. "Stevie here was lying when he told you about the man who dared him!"

This caused a mild stir.

"Was he indeed?" the dog-faced man asked, eyeing my sidekick with an expression that looked almost hungry.

"I was not!" Stewie yelped. "Why would you say that?!"

"Because your story doesn't hold up," I said with satisfaction. "There aren't many species that could do what you described without having left footprints, and all of them are conspicuous enough that it's not believable you didn't notice anything specific. I suspect you were deliberately describing that supposed individual in as vague terms as possible so as to attempt to not get caught in a lie when the culprit was found. And then there's the general silliness of your story in the first place, which requires you to have had no common sense whatsoever. Well?"

"No, I —!" Stevie began furiously. But then he looked at the stern-faced police officers, then over at me, then at the steely-eyed vampires standing beside him. His shoulders slumped. "Okay, fine," he muttered. "There was nobody else out there. I just wanted her to let me leave."

"Why were you in my house?" I demanded.

"The door was open," he said. "I was cold. I figured, why not sit in a warm house for awhile?"

I stared at him incredulously. "You do remember what I said before about your story being implausible because your actions lacked common sense?"

"Well, I'm sorry if I have no common sense!" he flared. "I had a long walk ahead of me, and it was cold!"

"You said the door was open," one of the police officers said. "Why would a specter need to open a door?"

"Maybe she left it open," Sidney said, pointing at me. "She has a terrible memory."

"I would not have left it open!" I said, scandalized. "It's possible I might have left it unlocked. But open, never!"

"You might have left it slightly ajar and not noticed," the man with the dog face said gently. "The wind could have blown it open further. That sort of thing happens to senior citizens."

This senior citizen was just about ready to feed him his own hat. This senior citizen was not a fan of condescension.

"I'm sorry I lied." Sidney looked at me guiltily, twitching the scarf around his neck. "But really, I didn't think anything had been stolen from your house. I just wanted you to let me go home. You were one freaky scary dodo, staring at me out in the snow."

"Apology and compliment accepted," I said stiffly. "But you've done irreparable damage to my case. Because of you, I wasted my time checking footprints. Because of you, the culprit had more time to escape!"

"The culprit probably escaped hours before you ever woke up," Steven shot back. "Even the crash that woke you up had nothing to do with it. It was just a bunch of trash cans falling over!"

"You don't know that that was unrelated!" I yelled.

"I *do!* You said so yourself! Or did you forget that, along with everything else?!"

"Tell you what," said the police officer who hadn't spoken yet. He was a tall man with antlers. "Why don't the two of you go back to your house, and when we're through here, we'll send someone over to take your statements. An *honest* one, this time," he added, giving my sidekick a rather frightening glare.

Sonny gulped and looked cowed.

I knew when I was being dismissed, and I didn't like it. But there didn't seem to be much point in trying to change their minds.

"Come on, then, Siegfried," I said. "Let's go back to my home."

"Out in the cold again?" he complained. But he didn't put up any more fuss. He looked a little bit afraid of the antlered man.

The Vampireclanaswangs were only too glad to see the back of us. Lillian even asked for her scarf back, to Sonny's dismay.

As we headed back towards my house, I stomped through the snow, frustrated that I was still being treated like a hindrance rather than a help to the investigation.

Had they even considered the most interesting aspect of all about a haltija having done it? A haltija wouldn't even have needed to open the safe. They just could have reached through the wall, made the turning stone insubstantial, and pulled it out. Nobody would have even been the wiser until they had tried to open the safe and found it gone.

Unless there was a specter alarm in there, which there probably was, I realized. *The thief would have needed to be substantial when he reached in there, or else he would have tripped it.*

Specter alarms were highly sensitive devices that would go off at the slightest touch. A specter turned them insubstantial before arming them, and once they were armed, they would go off if brushed even slightly by anything insubstantial later. Substantial things couldn't touch them and therefore wouldn't trigger them, so they were not an inconvenience to the person who wanted to keep their things protected.

I had only just remembered that those things existed. I was suddenly glad I hadn't brought up the curiosity of a haltija having chosen to break the safe in order to reach in with a substantial hand, because the police probably would've given me that same flat stare that said, "Why are you telling us obvious things?"

I shuffled down the sidewalk as the snow fell thicker, feeling depressed. What was the point of me being a sleuth if I couldn't help to solve my own mystery? Yet again, I was the incompetent shuffled off to the side so that I wouldn't get in anyone else's way. Yet again, I was nothing but silly old Aunt Dodo.

A car drove down the street, headlights bright through the white clumps raining down from above. It was driving slowly, but still faster than Sven and me, who were getting slower and slower as our visibility receded.

The car slowed to a stop, and a window opened. "Hey, need a ride?" the driver called from inside.

"No, thank you!" I said. "We're fine."

"Y-yep, we're fine!" Severus agreed.

"Your teeth are chattering," the man said in exasperation. "That doesn't look fine."

"It's only a two-minute walk," I said. "Don't worry."

"Can you even see where you're going?" he asked.

The wind took that moment to pick up, gusting more snow at us. I stared out into white-speckled darkness. He might have a point. I couldn't see more than a few feet in front of my face. Had I forgotten which way my house was?

"Get in," the driver said, pushing a button. There was a sound of doors unlocking. "Nobody should be out on a night like this."

Stormy didn't wait. He pulled open the back door and dove into the car. He blew on his hands to warm them.

"Get in," the driver told me.

"No thanks," I said. "We'll be fine on our own."

He pulled out a gun and leveled it at me. "Get in."

I had a terrible feeling that things had gone very wrong.

CHAPTER
I'm Sure I'll Remember It

estled inside the warm car, Severus blew on his hands while I sat in the back beside him, stiff with terror. The car started up, and it began to crawl down the road.

"Wh-where are we going?" I stammered.

"I don't know," the driver said succinctly. "I guess that depends on how much you've figured out."

"Nothing at all," Stanley said quickly. "She's a terrible sleuth."

I was not impressed with his loyalty.

"I'm a wonderful sleuth, but I have no idea who you are," I said coldly. "Since you've kidnapped us at gunpoint, maybe you'd be so kind to elucidate us."

He glanced back at us in the rearview mirror, grinned, and said nothing.

"Well, obviously you're the haltija who stole my turning stone," I said crossly. "Most likely you were listening to our conversation from a listening device, or maybe you were hiding under our feet after the police left. Either way, I clearly said something that alarmed you, so I must have figured out something you don't want the police to know."

The driver just grinned.

"That, or you want them to *think* I figured out something you don't want them to know," I added. "To send them barking up the wrong tree. Or I'm just a generic hostage."

"Two hostages," Stormy muttered.

"You really must stop whining," I said reprovingly. "At least you're warm now. That's what you wanted, right?"

"I'd like to *live*, too!"

"Tell me what else you know," the man from the driver's seat said sharply.

"Don't say a word!" Severus hissed.

I ignored my sidekick. "Of course. But first, a question."

"Absolutely not," the man said succinctly. "You're talking. I'm the one with the gun."

So much for the villainous monologue I'd been hoping for.

"What are you going to do with us?" I demanded.

"That's a question. I'm not answering those."

I worked backward, trying to figure out what I might have said in the recent past to make this man alarmed enough to kidnap me. What could possibly be worth showing me his face?

Unless it wasn't his face, of course. Unless he was an aswang. They could shapeshift into anybody they sucked blood from.

My mind worked feverishly. Hadn't Libby mentioned that some members of their clan wanted to get work turning people a second time, which was currently illegal? And hadn't Braeden disapproved? Perhaps one of them, knowing that their clan leader wouldn't allow it, had decided to take matters into his own hands. Perhaps he'd stolen the turning stone to force their clan to merge with another one with a clan leader more favorable to his interests.

But in that case, where was the haltija? Was he — or she — back at the Vampireclanaswangs' house, listening to the police?

There was only one way to find out. I checked the pockets of my bathrobe and found a ball of lint. I threw it at the back of his head.

He flicked insubstantial in the space of a flinch. Then he was back to normal, and roared, "What was that for?!"

"Just testing," I said.

"Testing what?!"

"To see whether you were a haltija or not. You had pointed ears while insubstantial, so I assume you are. I thought maybe you were an aswang. Do you have any conspirators, or did you work alone? I'd like my turning stone back now, please."

Sigmund moaned and put his face in his hands. He seemed to be mumbling something like, "We're gonna die . . ."

"I'm not answering any questions!" our captor roared. "You tell me what you know, *now!*"

Siegfried looked completely ashen. His pasty skin was even whiter than usual.

"Don't worry," I reassured him. "He's probably planning to kill us anyway. We've seen his face."

Siegfried looked incredulous and not at all reassured.

"TALK!" our captor roared.

We reached an intersection and a car crossed in front of us, bright headlights flashing. Our driver clutched the steering wheel with both hands and shouted obscenities at the car that had zoomed past us at a dangerous speed.

Well, he was distracted, so . . .

I shifted to half-form, jabbed my extra-long neck forward, and grabbed the gun in my teeth. Then I leapt back and shifted to dodo, hiding the gun inside me.

"HEY!" the driver screamed, spinning around.

I flapped my wings and quacked gleefully.

"I can still wring your neck," he snarled, going insubstantial.

I might have made a slight tactical error.

I dove for the front seat, but he was already back here with us. He seized my fragile dodo neck. I slashed at his face with my talons, he flinched insubstantial, and I scrambled the rest of the way into the front.

Behind me, Skittles was screaming, and I glanced back to see a vicious fight between a skinny little twig and bulky man who could go insubstantial. It wasn't a fair fight at all. So I shifted to half-form and pressed my own advantage.

Or rather, the gas pedal.

The car lurched forward, skidded, fishtailed, and went spinning out of control.

The haltija yelled and hung on to the seat. For a split second, I wondered why he didn't just go insubstantial, but realized that he didn't want the car to leave him behind.

"Brake!" Skittles screamed. "Brake! Brake! Brake!"

A brake wouldn't help. I knew that for sure. I'd driven on icy roads before. So I did the one thing that seemed sensible. I reached for my seat belt and slammed it into the buckle.

WHAM!

The car rammed straight into a cement barrier at the side of the road. Our abductor went flying. My head snapped forward and back again. Spaghetti screamed.

I now felt dizzy. Was the car tilting? No, maybe it was whiplash. Ow . . .

Spaghetti was still screaming.

"Stop screaming!" I yelled. "What's going on back —"

I looked. My breath caught, and bile rose in my throat.

Our captor was the only one who hadn't been wearing a seat belt, and his head had smashed straight through the window beside him.

He should have gone insubstantial, I thought numbly.

I shifted to human form to feel my neck and see how bad the injury was, found the gun I'd forgotten about between my teeth, and spat it out into my pocket to deal with later.

My sidekick was still screaming.

I noticed that the man's chest was rising and falling, even though there was a terrifying amount of blood coming from his head wound. I let out a long, shuddering breath. "Sousaphone, stop screaming. Call the police."

"But — but — but —!" the boy gibbered.

"911! Police! Ambulance! Now!"

He yanked a phone out of his pocket, dropping it several times because his hands were shaking, and finally managed to dial.

Five minutes later that felt more like five years, we were rescued. A specter EMT made the car insubstantial while a basajaun pulled us out, and a dracula EMT sliced his wrist to produce vampire blood.

"Here," he ordered us, handing us each a paper cup that was about a quarter full. "Drink it." His wrist had healed in less than ten seconds.

"Ewww," Steven moaned, but he did so. I did the same.

In a few minutes, we were both fine. All our injuries were healed. Our captor, however, was another story.

"Can't you heal him, too?" I asked nervously as the basajaun and specter loaded him up on a stretcher. A police officer who had arrived shortly after the ambulance was talking with them.

"We can," the vampire said shortly, "but we've only given him a few drops to stabilize him. If your story's true, he's a violent criminal, and in cases of violent criminals, we prefer not to heal them entirely until they're safely behind bars."

"What if our story *weren't* true?" Stewie asked.

"Then you'd face obstruction of justice charges, and possibly a charge for reckless endangerment of human or person life," the EMT said shortly. "Excuse me."

The police waved and wandered over to us as the ambulance took off, its sirens blaring.

"You're a really bad driver," Sterling joked, laughing shakily.

"I'm a *wonderful* driver," I said. "I'm just not very good at finding where I'm going. And I lost my car keys two weeks ago."

He laughed, as if I had been joking.

"Shall I drop you off at home?" the police officer asked, reaching us. "I assume you won't be driving." He looked pointedly at the totaled car.

"Yes, please," I said with a weak smile. "That would be great."

"Who shall I take home first? Or do you live together?"

"Oh, take Spaghetti home first," I said quickly, gesturing at the boy. "He's been wanting to go back home all night. And now that the case has been solved . . ."

My sidekick gave me a rueful look. "Sebastian. That has got to be the weirdest one you've come up with yet."

"Regardless," I said, "tell the man your address."

Spaghetti started to speak, and then paused. "Actually, do you mind if I go back home with you?"

"Why?" I asked.
"Because I want more of that hot water you call tea."
My mouth fell open. "Did I forget to put the ginseng in?!"
"Yes, you did," he said, laughing.
"So *that's* why it was so flavorless!"
He guffawed.
"Well, this time I'll remember it," I said, flustered.
"Nah, hot water's fine," he grinned.

CHAPTER
I Think I Forgot It

He and I got out of the police car at my house, and we waved goodbye to the police officer who drove off.

"Did you really lose your car keys two weeks ago?" Seymour asked, eyeing the car parked in my driveway.

"Not to worry," I said. "I can grocery shop online."

He snorted.

I pulled my house keys out of my pocket, unlocked the door, and let us in. A blast of heat reminded me that I still hadn't turned down the heater from ninety degrees. I would really have to fix that before my gas bill became astronomical.

"Now, let's get that tea started," I said, bustling off towards the kitchen.

"Actually, maybe I'll just borrow a coat and go home," he said, glancing at the coat closet.

What a chicken, so afraid to try something new.

"Nonsense," I scolded. "You have to try it with the ginseng in it. It really does taste better that way."

"Maybe next time," he said.

"Maybe tonight," I said firmly. I held the kettle under the faucet of the kitchen sink and filled it up.

As I placed the kettle on the stovetop and turned it on, a sly smile crept across my face. He didn't know it yet, but I was going to convince that boy he wanted to be a dodo. Now that the criminal was caught, they'd find my turning stone soon enough, and what better way for Victoria to forgive me than to introduce her to a prospective new clan member?

Not that I was going to tell him that yet, of course. He was so determined to stay human, silly boy. He would have to be talked into it. But I was certain I could do it eventually.

I was almost glad I'd left the turning stone out on the table, rather than hiding it properly. If I hadn't done that, the thief who'd come to rob my neighbors' turning stone wouldn't have seen it, it wouldn't have been stolen as an impulsive extra prize, and I wouldn't have had this opportunity to make friends with a young person to add to our clan.

Plus, of course, the police clearly wouldn't have been able to solve this case without me. At very least, without me, the criminal would have escaped.

I headed to the hallway, where Simson was flipping through my the coats in my coat closet. He paused at a bright magenta woollen one with obvious distaste.

"Oh, that one's nice and warm," I said. "Would you like —"

"No."

I noticed that his clothes were damp, no doubt from sitting in a warm car after being snowed on. My clothes were damp, too, but I didn't have a walk through the snow ahead of me.

A thought occurred to me, and I hurried to the laundry room, where I found what I was looking for: a pair of jeans and T-shirt from one of my nephews visiting a few months ago. I'd done his laundry after he'd spilled soda all over himself, and I had kept forgetting to return the clothing to him.

"Here," I said, returning to the hallway with the clothes slung over my arm. "You'll be much more comfortable in dry clothes."

"No, I'll be fine," he said, looking over a thick black coat.

"Going outside in wet things?" I scolded. "I don't think so! You'll catch your death of cold!"

"Look, I'm fine!"

"You are not fine!"

"I don't need them!"

"You will wear them!"

He was being stubborn, so I seized the shoulder of his damp shirt and shifted to half-form to make it disappear.

"HEY!" he screamed, grabbing the dry clothes from me.

But not before I'd seen.

"Why . . . do you have feathers on your chest?" I asked slowly.

"It's a costume," he snapped, yanking on my nephew's T-shirt with rapid speed.

"That is not a costume," I said. "That is a half-form."

"It's not a half-form," he said furiously. "I told you, I'm human."

"Then why do you have grey feathers?" I shot back. "What kind of werebird are you? Why would you lie about that? What possible reason —"

I stopped abruptly. Everything fell still.

"Give me back my turning stone."

"It's not yours anymore. It belongs to the cuckoo clan."

"GIVE ME BACK MY TURNING STONE!"

"You weren't using it!" he snapped. "We need another one!"

"Then *buy* one! Do you desperately want a bunch of weredodos in your clan?!"

"We don't have to worry about that!" he yelled. "We can change any stone to cuckoo just by using it once! That's our magical ability!"

I felt like I was going to faint.

"Look, I'm sorry," he said, edging off to the side. "You've been really nice, and I appreciate that you let me come here so the cops wouldn't know where I live, but I've got to get going now."

"You were working with him all along," I said, hyperventilating. "You called that haltija to pick us up!"

"Only because you said you'd had a breakthrough!" he said defensively. "And then you wouldn't say what it was! I thought you were doing that thing where you gather all the suspects and then reveal who —"

"How did you call him without me noticing?!"

"I texted him!" he said, exasperated, pulling out his phone and wiggling it in front of me. "It's this newfangled invention that people your age really ought to learn how to —"

I lunged for the phone and grabbed it. I shifted to dodo, taking the phone inside me, and shifted back to half-form again.

"STOP STEALING MY THINGS!" Stormy yelled.

"I could say the same thing!" I shot back. "Now, do you really think the police can't use that phone to find you if I hand it to them?"

His face turned bright red. "Come on, lady! It was supposed to be a victimless crime!"

"Is that so?" I asked icily. "Speaking as one of your victims, you may have forgotten about the clan you were planning to destroy. Not to mention that little matter of the forcible abduction."

"I didn't know that guy was going to get violent!" Slater cried. "I just asked him to wait as an escape driver in case I needed it!"

"Astonishing," I said. "Imagine, a criminal getting violent."

"I only hired him in the first place because there was security at your clan leader's house! I was planning to nab the stone while she was on vacation. I didn't know she was going to hand it over to somebody who doesn't even lock the back door. As soon as I saw that I could just stroll in and grab it, I called the guy and told him I didn't need his help anymore. I didn't know he was going to improvise and steal somebody else's turning stone instead!"

So that meant my clan's turning stone had been the original target, and not an afterthought? In a sense, I was proud. It was nice that our clan had been valued, for once.

Of course, that didn't mean I was going to let him keep it.

"Turning stone," I said, pointing at the ground. "Or I will call the police. I'm sure they'd be delighted to have your phone."

"Maaaaaan," he complained, shifting to human form. A backpack bulged out of his shoulder, and he opened it to pull out a green, glowing stone. He thumped it on the floor and glowered at me. "You really don't fight fair, old bat."

"I am not a bat," I said. "I am a dodo."

And I was also a sleuth. One who had just saved my clan's turning stone.

". . . And so you have it," I finished, passing a platter of cookies from Victoria to Anabel. "That's how I saved the day from that scoundrel named Silvester."

"You almost *ruined* the day by leaving the door unlocked," Victoria said sourly. She wasn't easy to please. "I can't believe I trusted you to watch over it."

"Oh, hush up," Anabel said, taking several cookies. She was the oldest of us and also the most energetic, despite being over eighty. She refused to retire. She taught yoga and enjoyed it too much. "It sounds like it would have been stolen anyway, and she saved it."

"But all the same, when I entrusted —!"

"I can't wait until my next case!" I broke in. There was no point in letting Victoria jump on a soapbox. "It's just a shame I don't have a magical ability. Like tracking magic! It would be so useful for all the sleuthing I'm going to do."

Anabel and Victoria exchanged looks.

"What?" I asked.

"You *have* a magical ability," Victoria said with exasperation.

"I do?"

"Yes! It's the same one we have!"

I stared at her blankly.

Anabel reached forward and dropped a cookie into thin air. It disappeared.

"Ohhhhhhhhhhhhhhhh!" I cried. "MY POCKET!"

I reached into my air pocket and pulled out my phone, my wallet, six notebooks, eight pens, two scribbled-on stacks of Post-It Notes, two phone bills, one utility bill, the gun that had gone missing after the accident, and my car keys.

I picked them up and dangled them in front of me.

"Another mystery solved!" I said triumphantly.